Little Polar Bear

A Little Animal Adventure

Little
Polar Bear

Written by Ariane Chottin
Adapted by Mary Connell and Suzanne G. Beason
Illustrations by Catherine Nouvelle

Published by The Reader's Digest Association Limited
London ❖ New York ❖ Sydney ❖ Montreal

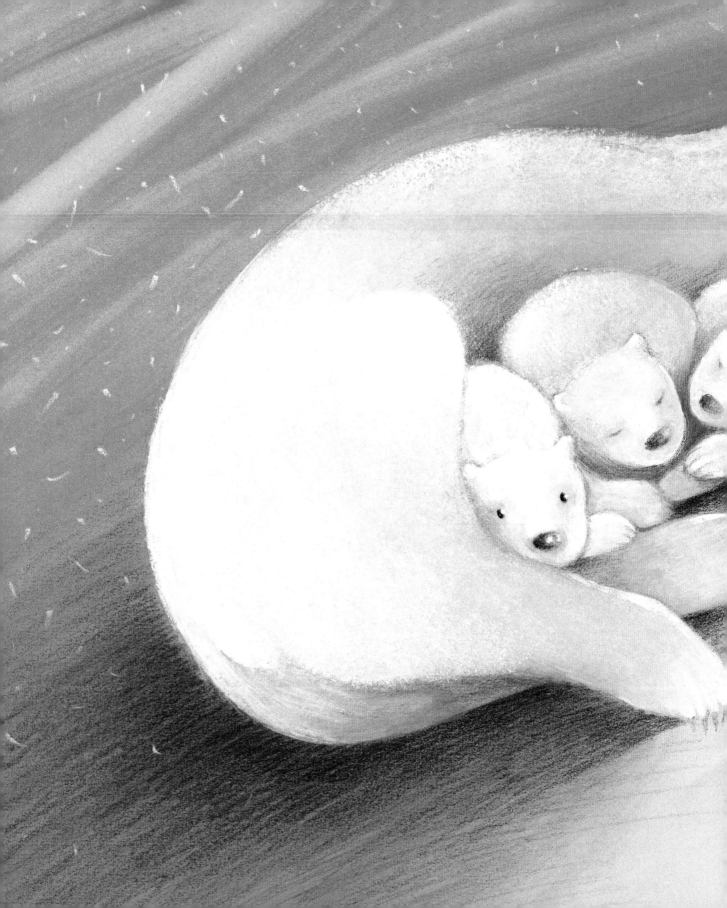

Nestled down in their den of snow,
Mother Polar Bear and her baby cubs were
fast asleep. They snuggled together, pure
white bundles of fur, warm and cosy in
their underground home.

The fierce winter wind that blew
outside couldn't reach them. Golden rays
of sunshine were beginning to filter through
the ice above them. Spring was coming!

One by one, the cubs woke up. It was time for their very first swim! Ernest and his sisters crept cautiously out of their den, following their mother across the snow to where ice had become freezing water.

'Don't be afraid! Just go ahead and dive in,' said Mother Polar Bear.

The three little bears peered anxiously into the dark water.

'One, two, three - in you go!' urged their mother and the three dived bravely into the sea.

Ernest, who was the smallest of the three, scrambled straight out again. He shook himself and started to cough.

'That water was icy! It was terrible!' he grumbled. 'Is there nothing to do around here except swim in this freezing ocean? I don't have any friends and I'm really bored,' he added rudely.

Ernest lay down on a block of ice and began to moan. He didn't notice a little white arctic fox, who was creeping quietly towards him.

'Don't be so sad, Little Polar Bear,' said Baby Fox. 'There are all kinds of animals in this big white world for you to play with. They're just so white that it's hard to spot them! Would you like to come with me? I'll introduce you to them.'

Just then, a sudden sound made the two new friends turn around. A pair of big black eyes were staring at them. It was a baby seal!

'Hello, Snowy!' called Baby Fox. 'Don't be afraid of my new friend, Little Polar Bear. He just wants to get to know you.'

'That little seal is so white!' exclaimed Ernest.
'That's true but in three weeks' time his fur
coat will change to a silver colour. Then he'll look
just like his parents,' said Baby Fox.
He darted ahead of them, shouting impatiently,
'Come on, let's play!'

Next, Madame Owl, a glamorous Great White Owl, swooped down and perched between the two friends.

'Hello, Baby Fox. Hello, Little Polar Bear. Have either of you, by any chance, heard any mice scurrying across the ice? I have to feed my fledglings and I'm in a hurry!'

'No, we haven't. But where do you live?' asked Ernest.

'In the far north, just like you do. But I live in the forest and build my nest in an old hollow tree,' replied the fine bird. Then she flew silently away.

'Her feathers are arranged in a special pattern so that she can fly without making a sound,' explained Baby Fox.

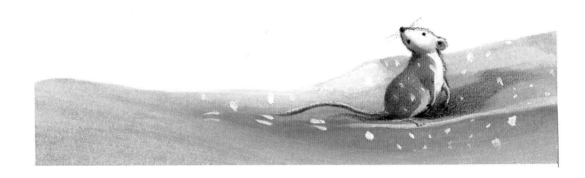

A little farther on, Little Polar Bear and Baby Fox spotted a slim and elegant white figure sliding across the ice.

'Who's that,' called Baby Fox. A perfect tiny triangular face popped up.

'Who are you, dear little creature?' Ernest asked politely.

'I'm Miss Ermine,' replied the little animal
as she bounded away. 'I'm as white as snow and
I have exquisite fur!'
    'How lovely you are!' said Little Polar Bear.

But Little Polar Bear was getting tired. He sat down and sighed. 'Do we still have a long way to go?' he asked. 'How many more white creatures live nearby?'

'Well, there's the Snow Partridge,' said Baby Fox. 'He has brown feathers in summer and white ones in winter. And then there's also the Polar Rabbit. His paws are so wide that he can run without sinking into the powdery snow. We call him Snowshoe Rabbit.'

It was time to go home. Mother Polar Bear and Ernest's little sisters had already returned to the den.

'Hello!' called Baby Fox to Little Polar Bear's family. 'Nice to meet you but please excuse me. I live over there in a much smaller den with my family. I'll see you again, very soon.'

'Goodbye, for now', Little Polar Bear called to his friend. Then he slid down the long ice corridor that led to his underground den.

Mother Bear had left a nice warm spot for her mischievous son. Ernest snuggled up next to her furry coat and fell fast asleep, dreaming about all his new friends and the wonderful snowy world in which they lived.

All about ...
POLAR BEARS

ICE BEARS

Polar bears live on icebergs at the North Pole. They are sea mammals. They eat fish and seals and spend most of their time in the water.

SEAL-SPOTTING

Polar bears can be very patient. They have been known to sit for hours beside a hole in the ice, waiting for an unsuspecting seal to pop up.

FACT FILE

FAT AND FUR
Polar bears have a layer of fat under their skin that helps them to stay warm. Their fur coat is also very thick and keeps out water.

Did you know?

SLEEP TIGHT

Polar bears hibernate. They go into their dens at the beginning of winter and then fall into a deep sleep. The mother polar bear gives birth to her cubs during this time.

FISHY DISHES

Before going into hibernation, polar bears devour fish, seaweed, shellfish and seals in order to store up enough fat to last them all winter.

BARE BABIES

Baby polar bears are very tiny at birth. They can't see and they have no fur. They grow very rapidly. By the time they are three months old, they weigh about 3 kilos.

YOUNG FAMILIES

Little Polar Bear is a Little Animal Adventures book
published by Reader's Digest Young Families, Inc.
by arrangement with Éditions Nathan, Paris, France

Written by Ariane Chottin
Adapted by Mary Çonnell and Suzanne G. Beason
Illustrations by Catherine Nouvelle
Notebook artwork © Paul Bommer

Copyright © 1990 Éditions Nathan, Paris, France
Édition originale: *En Avant, Petit Ours Blanc!*
All rights reserved.

This edition was adapted and published in 2008 by
The Reader's Digest Association Limited
11 Westferry Circus, Canary Wharf, London E14 4HE

We are committed to both the quality of our products
and the service we provide to our customers.
We value your comments, so please feel free to contact us on
08705 113366 or via our website at:
www.readersdigest.co.uk
If you have any comments or suggestions about the content of our books,
you can contact us at:
gbeditorial@readersdigest.co.uk

Printed in China

Book code: 637-012 UP0000-2
ISBN: 978 0 276 44239 1